Not Yet

Lisa Cox & Lori Hockema

First published by Dog Ear Publishing
4011 Vincennes Rd
Indianapolis, IN 46268
www.dogearpublishing.net

ISBN: 978-1-4575-5563-3

This book is printed on acid-free paper.

This book is a work of fiction. Places, events, and situations in this book are purely fictional and any resemblance to actual persons, living or dead, is coincidental.

Printed in the United States of America

I wake up every morning

to a fresh and brand-new day.

Sometimes I make mistakes.

Mom says,

"Lorisa, that's OK."

Doodle, you're an awesome dog even when you make a mess.

Mom tells us,

"Just clean it up and keep doing your best."

I put my power bracelet on before I go to school.
It reminds me to believe in me, and it really looks so cool.

As I walk out to the bus, my mom shouts out to me,

"Lorisa, you can do all things. You have many possibilities!"

Am I there? Not Yet!

I'll get there. You bet!

I walk into my classroom where I make my dreams come true.
Oops! Before I start the first task, I must tie my shoe.

Someday I'll climb a mountain,
but now it's way too big for me.

I'll sail across the ocean

with its waves so wild and free.

I will learn a different language, so I can better understand.

Yes

I will stand up
for what's right,
reach out,
and help new friends.

Am I there? Not Yet!

I'll get there. You bet!

I will work with scientists and help cure the yucky cold.

Maybe I'll become a vet and take care of Doodle when she's old.

I'll do my part to help make this world a cleaner place to play.

I'll learn to grow a garden
and give the food away.

Am I there? Not Yet!

I'll get there. You bet!

If the answers are hard to find and cause me to sweat, I will keep trying and not whine or fret.

When I look back on each day, I will see sometimes I win.
I know there will be times I lose, but I will always try again.

The school day is over. I'm home now;
I can rest. First, I feed my Doodle dog.
Oops! I tried my best.

Am I there? Not Yet!

I'll get there. You bet!

Before I fall asleep, I look at the moon each night.
It looks too far to ever reach, but it's such a wonderful sight.

I think about the astronauts who made their dreams come true. They did not quit. They walked on it. I have some big dreams, too.

Each day I wear my bracelet. "Not Yet" is what it says.
These two words keep me strong. I hear them in my head.
I will keep working every day and never forget……..

Am I there? Not Yet!

I'll get there. You bet!

What is in your dream bubble?

Are you there? Not yet!

You'll get there. You bet!

What is in your dream bubble?

Are you there?   Not yet!

You'll get there. You bet!!

What is in your dream bubble?

Are you there? Not yet!

You'll get there. You bet!!

9 781457 555633